Big People, Little People

Malachy Doyle
Illustrated by Mark Chambers

A & C Black • London

For Naomi, Hannah and Liam – my very own big little people

White Wolves series consultant: Sue Ellis,
Centre for Literacy in Primary Education

This book can be used in the White Wolves Guided Reading
programme by more advanced readers in Year 2

First published 2009 by
A & C Black Publishers Ltd
36 Soho Square, London, W1D 3QY

www.acblack.com
www.malachydoyle.com

Text copyright © 2009 Malachy Doyle
Illustrations copyright © 2009 Mark Chambers

The rights of Malachy Doyle and Mark Chambers to be identified
as the author and illustrator of this work has been asserted by them
in accordance with the Copyrights, Designs and Patents Act 1988.

ISBN 978-1-4081-1236-6

A CIP catalogue for this book is available from the British Library.

This book is produced using paper that is made from wood
grown in managed, sustainable forests. It is natural, renewable
and recyclable. The logging and manufacturing processes conform
to the environmental regulations of the country of origin.

Printed and bound in China by C&C Offset Printing Co.

Chapter One

"Who is the richest king in the world?" cried King Iubdan.

"You!" roared the Little People.

"Who is the most powerful king in the world?" cried King Iubdan.

"You!" roared the Little People.

All except one. Ossian, the royal minstrel, was clutching his sides, laughing.

"How dare you, Minstrel!" shouted the king. "Your job is to sing, not laugh."

"I'm sorry, Your Majesty," said Ossian. "It's just so funny to hear you boasting about how rich and powerful you are, when I know a land where even the *babies* are stronger."

"How rude this man is!" stormed the king. "Guards! Throw him in prison!"

"But it is the truth, my lord," cried Ossian, as the guards dragged him away. "Give me three days and I will prove it."

Princess Dana stepped forward. "Do as he asks, Father," she begged. "Just to show how generous you are."

"All right, you have three days, Ossian," said the king. "Then you can kiss goodbye to your family and freedom.

Chapter Two

Ossian pushed and shoved, shoved and
pushed, and at last the Gigantic Pebble
rolled to one side.

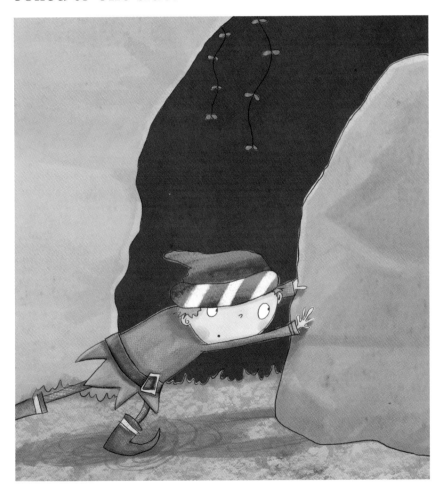

Up he climbed, up the many steps, until he reached the place where Little People had never been allowed to go.

The place that Little People didn't even know existed.

The land of the Big
People.

Ossian had been
there, of course. That's
where he'd seen the child.
A child who was bigger
than the tallest man in
his land.

But he'd never told
anyone, not even his
mother. For he knew that
no one would believe him.
And he knew he'd get
into all sorts of trouble.

Over land and water he raced, through ferns and forest, for a night and a day, until he came to the palace of Fergus, the king of the Big People.

Ossian knocked on the door
and waited. He knocked a bit
harder and waited. Then he
banged and he thumped and
at last the door opened.

"Who's there?" boomed
a voice.

"Me," squeaked Ossian.

"Where?" said the guard.

"Down here!"
cried Ossian.

So the guard picked him up and carried
him into the Great Hall.

Chapter Three

"Is it a mouse? Is it a puppet?"

The lords and ladies crowded around and Ossian was terrified.

But Neddy Bug, the king's son, felt sorry for the little fellow. He bent down, scooped Ossian up and took him, in the palm of his hand, to his father.

"Are you real?" asked King Fergus. "Really real? For I've never seen anyone as small as you before."

"I'm Ossian, minstrel to King Iubdan of the Little People," squeaked Ossian. "And I've never seen anyone as big as *you* before!"

"A minstrel, indeed!" said the king, who was a lover of music. "Give us a song, then."

"But I have to get home to my own king at once!" said Ossian. "I have three days to bring him proof that you and your people exist, or he'll throw me in prison."

King Fergus became angry. He wasn't used to people disobeying him. "Sing, I said, or I'll throw you in prison *here*!"

Ossian had no choice, so he cleared his throat and sang.

When he'd finished, everyone clapped. But the noise was so loud that Ossian had to cover his ears.

"So, little fellow," said the king. "Where are you from? Tell me about your land."

"I can't do that," said Ossian. "My king would be furious. But if you allow your son to come back with me, he'll tell you all about it when he returns."

"Please, Father! Please!" cried Neddy Bug.

And the king agreed.

Chapter Four

So off they went, Neddy Bug and Ossian,
through the ferns and forest. They made
their way down the many steps and out past
the Gigantic Pebble.

"Ossian's back!" yelled the Little People.
"He's brought a giant with him!"

King Iubdan and Princess Dana came out
to see them.

"Why have you brought this giant to kill
us?" cried the king, taking out his sword.

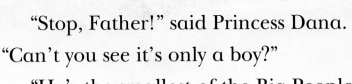

"Stop, Father!" said Princess Dana. "Can't you see it's only a boy?"

"He's the smallest of the Big People, Your Majesty," said Ossian. "I brought him here to prove what I told you before was true. There *is* a land where even the babies are stronger than us!"

Neddy Bug stepped forward.

"I won't hurt you, my lord," he said. "I won't hurt anyone. I'm quite a small person in my own land, you see. I just wanted to see what a whole world of little people was like."

"And what *is* it like?" asked the king.

Neddy Bug looked all around him.

"It's lovely," he smiled.

King Iubdan was much happier then.

"Why don't you go and see what it's like in my world, Your Majesty?" said Neddy Bug. "I could stay here until you return."

And the king agreed.

So the next morning, Princess Dana and King Iubdan pushed past the Gigantic Pebble and climbed up the many steps. Then they rode on horseback, through ferns and forest, for a day and a night.

It was early when they arrived at the palace of King Fergus, and even the guards were asleep.

"I'm hungry," said King Iubdan. "And I can smell porridge…"

They crept through the gates and followed the smell to the kitchen. The king climbed on a chair, scrambled up on to the table, took a running jump at the porridge pot, and fell straight in.

"Help!" he cried. "I'm stuck!"

Princess Dana could do nothing to help but, at long last, the cook arrived.

"Aargh!" she cried.
"There's a rat in the
porridge!"

"It's not a rat," said
Princess Dana. "It's
my father!"

"Aargh!" cried the cook. "Another rat!"

"I'm a king, you silly woman," cried King
Iubdan. "Now get me out of here!"

So the cook pulled him out of the
porridge and took them to her master.

Chapter Five

"Well, well, well…" said King Fergus. "The king of the Little People! What were you doing, splashing about in my breakfast?"

"I was hungry," said King Iubdan. "I fell in."

King Fergus sighed. "As I am the kindest and most powerful king in the world, I shall forgive you."

"I'm afraid you are wrong," said King Iubdan. "It is I, King Iubdan, who is the kindest and most powerful king in the world."

"You're not!"

"I am."

"You're not!"

"I am!"

"Oh, do stop arguing, you two!" sighed Princess Dana. "It seems to me that now we've met, we must learn to get along with each other. So, why don't I stay here and get to know the ways of the Big People?"

King Iubdan thought for a moment, and then said, "Yes, and why doesn't your son, Neddy Bug, stay in my land and get to know the ways of the Little People?"

So they did.

And the princess got bigger, living with
the Big People and doing Big People things.

And Neddy Bug found himself getting
smaller, living with the Little People and
doing Little People things.

So the next time they met, Neddy Bug
and Princess Dana were bigger than little
and littler than big, and there wasn't much
difference between them at all.

Then the strangest thing happened.
Neddy Bug and Princess Dana fell in love.

And in time, they got married. Ossian sang at the wedding and all the people, both Little and Big, were invited.

And in time, more time, Neddy Bug and Princess Dana had loads of children, who had loads of children, who spread across the land.

And that's why, these days, most of the people in Ireland are neither big nor little but somewhere in between, and happy enough at that.

So now you know.